John Burningham

Mr Gumpy's Motor Car

RED FOX

Some other books by John Burningham

Aldo

Avocado Baby

Borka

Cloudland

Come away from the water, Shirley

Courtney

Edwardo

Granpa

Harquin

Humbert

Husherbye

John Patrick Norman McHennessy

The Magic Bed

Mr Gumpy's Outing

Oi! Get off our Train

The Shopping Basket

Simp

Time to get out of the bath, Shirley

Trubloff

Whadayamean

Where's Julius?

Would you rather . . .

MR GUMPY'S MOTOR CAR
A RED FOX BOOK 978 1 849 41285 8

First published in Great Britain by Jonathan Cape,
an imprint of Random House Children's Books
A Random House Group Company

Jonathan Cape edition published 1973
Red Fox edition first published 2002
This edition with CD published 2011

10 9 8 7 6 5 4 3 2 1

Red Fox Books are published by Random House Children's Books,
61–63 Uxbridge Road, London W5 5SA

www.kidsatrandomhouse.co.uk
www.rbooks.co.uk

Addresses for companies within The Random House Group Limited can be found at:
www.randomhouse.co.uk/offices.htm

THE RANDOM HOUSE GROUP Limited Reg. No. 954009

A CIP catalogue record for this book is available from the British Library.

Printed in China

Mr Gumpy was going for a ride in his car.

He drove out of the gate and down the lane.

"May we come too?" said the children.

"May we?" said the rabbit, the cat, the dog, the pig, the sheep, the chickens, the calf and the goat.

"All right," said Mr Gumpy.
"But it will be a squash."

And they all piled in.

"It's a lovely day," said Mr Gumpy. "Let's take the old cart-track across the fields."

For a while they drove along happily. The sun shone, the engine chugged and everyone was enjoying the ride.

"I don't like the look of those clouds. I think it's going to rain," said Mr Gumpy.

Very soon the dark clouds were right overhead.
Mr Gumpy stopped the car. He jumped out,
put up the hood, and down came the rain.

The road grew muddier and muddier,
and the wheels began to spin.
Mr Gumpy looked at the hill ahead.

"Some of you will have to get out and push,"
he said.

"Not me," said the goat. "I'm too old."

"Not me," said the calf. "I'm too young."

"Not us," said the chickens. "We can't push."

"Not me," said the sheep. "I might catch cold."

"Not me," said the pig.
"I've a bone in my trotter."

"Not me," said the dog.
"But I'll drive if you like."

"Not me," said the cat. "It would ruin my fur."

"Not me," said the rabbit. "I'm not very well."

"Not me," said the girl. "He's stronger."

"Not me," said the boy. "She's bigger."

The wheels churned...

The car sank deeper into the mud.
"Now we're really stuck," said Mr Gumpy.
They all got out and pushed.

They pushed and shoved and heaved and strained and gasped and slipped and slithered and squelched.

Slowly the car began to move…

"Don't stop!" cried Mr Gumpy. "Keep it up! We're nearly there."

Everyone gave a mighty heave – the tyres gripped…

The car edged its way to the top of the hill.
They looked up and saw that the sun
was shining.

"We'll drive home across the bridge,"
said Mr Gumpy.
"There'll be time for a swim."

"Goodbye," said Mr Gumpy.
"Come for a drive another day."